Lulu the Big Little Chick

PAULETTE BOGAN

BLOOMSBURY

NEW YORK BERLIN LONDON

Published by Bloomsbury U.S.A. Children's Books
175 Fifth Avenue, New York, New York 10010

Library of Congress Cataloging-in-Publication Data
Bogan, Paulette.
Lulu the big little chick / by Paulette Bogan. — 1st U.S. ed.
p.   cm.
Summary: When Lulu gets tired of being told she is too little to do things,
she decides to go far, far away.
ISBN-13: 978-1-59990-343-9 • ISBN-10: 1-59990-343-1 (hardcover)
ISBN-13: 978-1-59990-344-6 • ISBN-10: 1-59990-344-X (reinforced)
[1. Size—Fiction. 2. Chickens—Fiction. 3. Domestic animals—Fiction.
4. Mother and child—Fiction.] I. Title.
PZ7.B6339Lu 2009   [E]—dc22   2008036222

The art was done in watercolor and inks
Typeset in Maiandra
Book design by Donna Mark

First U.S. Edition 2009
Printed in China by South China Printing Company, Dongguan City, Guangdong
2 4 6 8 10 9 7 5 3 (hardcover)
2 4 6 8 10 9 7 5 3 1 (reinforced)

All papers used by Bloomsbury U.S.A. are natural, recyclable products
made from wood grown in well-managed forests. The manufacturing processes
conform to the environmental regulations of the country of origin.

To my big little chicks,
Soph, Rach, and Lulu

Lulu was tired of being the littlest chick on the farm. She was too little to lay eggs. She was too little to climb the big fence. She was too little to play in the cornfield. But when Momma said, "Lulu, you are too little to go very far from me . . ."

. . . Lulu said, "NO. I am big and I am going far, far away."

"I see," said Momma slowly. "So you are going far, far away?"

"Yes," said Lulu. "Right now."

"Okay," said Momma. "Good-bye, Lulu."

And Lulu marched out the barn door.

"OINK, OINK. Where are you headed, little miss?" snorted Mrs. Pig.

"I am going far, far away," said Lulu.

Splat. Lulu was covered with mud.
"Sorry," giggled the piglet. "You're so little, I didn't see you!"

"This is not far, far away enough," said Lulu.

Momma called out, "Do you need help getting clean, Lulu?"

"NO," said Lulu. "I am going far, far away, by myself."

"Okay," Momma said. "Good-bye, Lulu."

"This looks like far, far away," Lulu said, stepping into the sheep pen.

"BAA, BAA," said the sheep. "Watch out, little one. We almost squished you!"

"This is not far, far away, anyway. Good-bye, sheep. Good-bye, Momma!" Lulu yelled. "I am really going this time."

"I know," Momma called. "You are going far, far away. Good-bye, Lulu."

"Far, far away, here I come," said Lulu.

"NEIGH," said the horse. "I almost stepped on you!

Where do you think you are going, little chick?"

Lulu looked up and up and up. "Far, far away?" she whispered.

"You are too little to go far, far away," the horse neighed.

Lulu hurried away . . . smack into the biggest cow she had ever seen.

"MOO, I almost chewed you up with this tasty grass," said the cow. "What are you doing here, little lady?"

Lulu answered in a very small voice, "I am going far, far away?"

"HA," said the cow. "You are too little to go far, far away!"

Lulu got up and ran as fast and as far as she could. She did not see the pigs or the sheep or the horse or that big cow . . . or Momma. Lulu gulped and said in a very tiny voice, "Uh-oh, I think I am far, far away now."

Then there was a terrible sound: CAW, CAW, CAW! A huge creature Lulu had never seen before was flying right over her head. Lulu could not move. She whispered to herself, "I am a big chick, I am a big chick, I am . . . LITTLE!"

She closed her eyes as the sound came closer and closer. And then . . .

. . . Momma scooped Lulu up in her arms. "Oh, my Lulu, I missed you! How was far, far away?"

"Momma?" said Lulu.

"Yes, my love?" said Momma.

"Momma, next time I go far, far away, I think I will take you with me."